My I Book

by Jane Belk Moncure

illustrated by Linda Hohag

THE CHILD'S WORLD

ELGIN, ILLINOIS 60120

Library of Congress Cataloging in Publication Data

Moncure, Jane Belk.
  My "L" book.

  (My first steps to reading)
  Rev. ed. of: My L sound box. © 1978.
  Summary: The things Little l chooses to put in his
box do not wish to stay there—the lambs, lizards,
lion, lobster, and leopard all leap out.
    1. Children's stories, American.   [1. Alphabet]
I. Hohag, Linda. ill.   II. Moncure, Jane Belk.   My L
sound box.   III. Title.   IV. Series: Moncure, Jane Belk.
My first steps to reading.
PZ7.M739Myl 1984   [E]   84-17540
ISBN 0-89565-285-4

Distributed by Childrens Press, 1224 West Van Buren Street,
Chicago, Illinois 60607.

My "I" Book

Little had a box.

He said, "I will fill my  box ."

He found leaves
and lizards. "In you go," he said.

Little looked behind logs.

He found lambs.
They were little lambs.

"Hi, lambs," said Little  .
"You must be
little lost lambs.

In you go."

Then Little came to a lake.

The lizards leaped out of the box.

Little  put them back.

"Stay here, lizards," he said.

Then he looked in the lake.

A lobster   was in the lake.

He put the lobster into his box...

carefully.

The lobster had pinchers!

Little saw a lighthouse.

The lantern
was not lit.

So he
climbed
up the
ladder.

He lit the lantern.

Just then . . .

Little  heard a loud roar.

A lion was
at the door.
It was a
little lion.

The lion licked him

and sat in his lap.

He gave the lion
a lollipop.

"I will put you
into my box,"
he said.

And he did.

Little  heard another loud roar.

A leopard was at the door.

The leopard
licked him

and sat in his lap.

Little gave the
leopard a lollipop.

He put the leopard
into his box.

Guess what happened?

The lobster pinched the leopard.
Then all the animals leaped out of the box.

Little

put the lobster
into a lobster pot
so it could not pinch!

Just then he heard a loud roar.

It was a locomotive.

It went, "Choo-choo."

lobster in lobster pot

logs and ladder

leaves and lizards

leopard licking lollipop

"Let's go for a long ride,"

lion and lambs

locomotive

he said. And they did.

More words with Little

lamp

letter

lime

lemon

light

lovebirds

ladybug

l

lettuce

llama

lark

lady

lock

lily

lifeguard

29